Jump
at the Sun
Fairy-tale Classics

Cinderella

Illustrated by John Kurtz

JUMP AT THE SUN/HYPERION BOOKS FOR CHILDREN
New York

Text copyright © 2004 by Jump at the Sun

Illustrations copyright © 2004 by John Kurtz

For my wife Sandrina, I love you. —J.K.

Printed in the United States of America
First Edition
1 3 5 7 9 10 8 6 4 2

This book is set in 18-point Cantoria.
Library of Congress Cataloging-in-Publication Data on file.
ISBN 0-7868-0955-8

Once
upon
a time...

…there lived a girl named Cinderella, who was very beautiful and very kind. She lived with her mean old stepmother and her two evil stepsisters.

She was not allowed out of the house except to tend the garden. So her only friends were the animals, who loved her because she was so kind to them.

Every day Cinderella's stepmother and stepsisters made her wipe the cinders from the fireplace and clean the house from top to bottom.

And every day they made Cinderella draw their baths, style their hair, iron their clothes, and help them dress.

One day a royal
messenger knocked on
their door.

"The king is having a
royal ball for the prince
tonight! Every girl in
the kingdom is invited,"
he announced.

"Every girl but *you*,
Cinderella!" laughed her
stepsisters.

So Cinderella got her
bucket and broom and
began her chores.

As Cinderella swept the cinders, the younger stepsister yelled, "Cinderella! Cinderella! Help me into my gown of silk and rubies!"

As Cinderella scrubbed the floors, the older stepsister yelled, "Cinderella! Cinderella! Help me into my gown of gold and diamonds!"

Soon the evil threesome were dressed and on their way. "We're off to the royal ball! If you were clean of cinders and had something to wear, Cinderella, you could go too!" said her mean old stepmother.

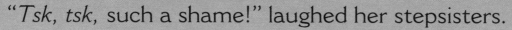

"*Tsk, tsk,* such a shame!" laughed her stepsisters.
"We're off to meet the prince," said one.
"One of us will be his wife!" said the other.

Cinderella ran to the garden and cried.
Slowly, a gentle wind of pixie dust and sparkles formed around her. Then someone appeared.
"Who—who are you?" Cinderella asked through her tears.

"I am your fairy godmother. And tonight, you *will* go to the royal ball and meet the prince!" said the woman.

"But how?" asked Cinderella.

"Make haste. I need five mice, a rabbit, and a pumpkin," said her fairy godmother. Cinderella didn't stop to ask why.

Cinderella called to the animals and they came quickly. Then she picked a pumpkin from the garden.

With a wave of her godmother's wand, the five mice became five sturdy horses, the pumpkin became a beautiful coach, and the rabbit became an elegant coachman.

Cinderella was wearing the gown of her dreams!
And tiny glass slippers sparkled on her dainty feet.
"Hurry to the ball!" said her fairy godmother.
"But you must return home before the clock strikes
twelve midnight! That is when my magic ends."

When Cinderella arrived at the ball, the prince could not take his eyes off her.

Everyone looked at the beautiful girl who had caught the eye of the handsome prince.

"May I have this dance?" he asked.

"Yes," said Cinderella.

And they danced. And they danced. And they danced. Until . . .

The clock rang out twelve times! Oh, no!
Cinderella remembered the words of her fairy
godmother: *You must return home before the clock
strikes twelve midnight!*

Cinderella ran out of the palace.

As she ran down the stairs, the prince found the tiny glass slipper she had left behind.

On her way home, everything turned back to normal: the pumpkin, the mice, the rabbit, and her dress.

Bong!

Bong!

Bong!

Bong!

Word traveled throughout the kingdom that the prince was looking for the girl whose foot could fit into the tiny glass slipper. He planned to ask for her hand in marriage!

When the prince arrived at Cinderella's home, each of her stepsisters tried but couldn't get one toe into the tiny glass slipper!

Then the prince saw Cinderella. He bent down on one knee and held out the slipper for her to try on. Her foot slipped right in. She and the prince both smiled.

"Finally, I have found you. Will you be my wife?" he asked.

Cinderella said, "Yes! I will!"
And they lived happily ever after.